THE PHANTOM CARWASH

*Lenny dreams of getting a carwash for
Christmas – a real carwash, full-size and in
working order. But he knows this is impossible.
However, Lenny's dream comes true when he
finds a carwash in the middle of a vacant patch.
But this is no ordinary carwash; however the
car goes in, it comes out transformed and reflecting
the nature of the person who drives it.
Eventually Father Christmas emerges and takes
Lenny on a magical journey.*

CHRIS POWLING

The Phantom Carwash

ILLUSTRATED BY SCOULAR ANDERSON

BARN OWL BOOKS

First published in Great Britain 1986
by Heinemann Young Books
This edition illustrated by Scoular Anderson
first published 2001 by Barn Owl Books
157 Fortis Green Road, London N10 3LX

Text copyright © Chris Powling 1986, 2001
Illustrations © Scoular Anderson 2001
The moral right of Chris Powling to be identified
as author and Scoular Anderson as illustrator
of this work has been asserted
ISBN 1 903015 13 8

A CIP catalogue record for this book
is available from the British Library

Designed and typeset by Douglas Martin Associates
Printed in China

For Jan, Kate and Ellie
My phantom carwashers

ONCE there was a boy called Lenny.
He lived in a part of London so
ordinary nobody ever noticed it.
Nobody ever noticed Lenny, either.
He had ordinary freckles and ordinary
hair and his grin was an ordinary grin.

Only one thing made Lenny special.
He wanted a carwash for Christmas.

'A what?' asked his Dad.

'A carwash,' said Lenny.

'They don't make them, son. Toy cars – yes. Or toy garages. But not a toy carwash.'

'I don't want a *toy* carwash, Dad. I want a *real* one.'

'A *real* carwash? What, up here in the flat?'

'We could put it out on the balcony,' said Lenny, hopefully.

His Dad laughed and so did his Mum.

'What about roller-blades?' they suggested. 'Or a computer? Or a football-game?'

'Thanks,' said Lenny. 'I'll have one of those instead.'

He said this because he didn't want to disappoint his Mum and Dad. Really, he wanted a carwash all the time.

'Why a carwash?' asked his Gran.

'I just like them,' Lenny said.

How could he explain? He shut his eyes and let a picture of a carwash come into his mind . . .

First the money goes clink in the slot and the carwash goes clunk all over. Then comes a spatter of water and a buzz of machinery. The brushes begin to turn. They look like giant spiders turning head-over-heels.

Help!

Are they creeping up on the car or is the car creeping up on them?

More water comes next. It pitter-patters on the bonnet and windscreen and side-windows and roof till the brushes catch up. After this comes a storm of spidery bristles pressing flat against the glass while the car shudders.

Suddenly it all stops.

And starts again just as suddenly. It's the same only backwards – pitter-patter and bristles, bristles and pitter-patter.

Too soon the carwash clunks to a halt. The car drips and glistens . . .

'You really do want a carwash for Christmas,' said Gran. 'I can tell by your face.'

'A football-game or a computer or a cowboy-outfit would be nearly as good,' said Lenny.

'How nearly?' Gran asked. '*Very*

nearly? Or not-so-nearly? Lenny
went red.

'Speak up,' said Gran.

'Not so nearly,' Lenny admitted.

'Ah, I thought as much. So it's a
carwash you're after. That would be
a full-size carwash in perfect working
order, I suppose?'

'If you could manage it, Gran.'

'*I* couldn't manage it, Lenny. I couldn't even afford the paper to wrap it up. But there is one person I can think of who might get one for you.'

'Who's that?'

'Come close and I'll whisper.'

Lenny went so close his ear was almost touching Gran's lips.

'Who?' he exclaimed.

'You heard,' said Gran.

'Santa Claus?' asked Lenny.

'Santa Claus,' insisted Gran. "Why, what's the matter?'

How could Lenny say he didn't believe in Santa Claus? His Gran would be so upset.

'Nothing,' said Lenny. 'I just . . . er . . . didn't think of him, that's all.'

'Well, now you *have* thought of him,' said Gran. 'So your problem's over. Happy Christmas.'

'Happy Christmas, Gran,' Lenny sighed.

Poor Lenny. He knew his Gran had been trying to help but now he felt worse than ever. For a moment he really had thought that when he woke up on Christmas morning he'd see a carwash at the foot of his bed, full-size and in perfect working order. He felt even sorrier for his Gran, though. Wouldn't you feel sorry for a grown-up who believes in an old man who rides through the sky and can visit millions and millions of

children in a single night by climbing down the chimney? Utterly daft! Why, some kids lived in places like Australia – Lenny himself had cousins who lived in a beach-house in Australia. Would they get a visit? And what about houses that haven't got chimneys? Lenny's own block of flats hadn't got a single chimney.

Santa Claus!

Lenny shook his head sadly.

For the next three weeks Lenny
went Christmas-shopping whenever
he could. He had saved his pocket-
money, emptied his money box and
thought hard. In the end he bought
cigars for Dad, a sparkly necklace
for Mum and a potted plant for
Gran. And slowly he got used to the

idea of having roller-blades or a
computer or a football-game for his
own present.

Except when he was asleep, that is.
Each night he dreamed of coins going
clink-clink-clink, of a spatter of water,
of a storm of bristles and of glistening
when it was over.

That year Christmas Eve was a Sunday. London was as quiet as it ever is. On the way home from his Sunday walk Lenny could hear his footsteps echoing along the street. The afternoon had grown dark and already there was a twinkle of fairy-lights in window after window. Lenny felt raindrops on his face.

'Wish it was snow,' he grumbled.

He pulled up the hood of his anorak and turned the corner. Here was the wasteground Lenny hated.

It was a sad, spooky place even
at midday but Lenny had to cross it
to get to the estate where he lived.
Usually he ran his fastest but this
time something made him stand as
still as a slot-machine when the
money runs out.

'It's a carwash,' he gasped. 'In the middle of the Dump! But . . . but it's different somehow . . .'

So it was. For example, where was the rest of the garage? This carwash had no forecourt, no petrol pumps, no air-line, no kiosk selling odds and ends for your car. A carwash was all there was.

Yet *what* a carwash! Even to an expert like Lenny it was splendid. The metalwork gleamed and the brushes were the biggest and bushiest he'd ever seen. Who owned it? When he moved closer he saw the notice. Its markings glowed in the twilight.

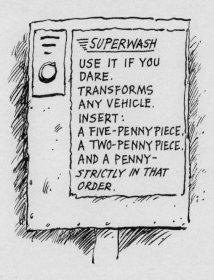

'Eight pence,' said a friendly voice. 'That's cheap.'

Lenny turned to see who it was.

Behind him stood a boy about twice as old as he was and about twice as tall. He wore a woollen bobble-hat and a matching scarf that muffled his voice.

'Reckon it works?' he asked.

'Should think so,' Lenny said.

'Reckon I could put this through it?'

The boy jerked his thumb at the bike he had been wheeling.

'A *bike*?' Lenny exclaimed.

'Well, it does say "transforms any vehicle". A bike's a vehicle, isn't it?'

'Suppose it is,' said Lenny.

'And you've got to admit this bike needs cleaning. Bought it as a Christmas present for my Dad. Three quid it cost me. Of course it wants doing up. Dad needs it to get to work. He'd prefer a racing-bike in his heart of hearts but you can't get one of those for three quid.'

'Suppose you can't,' said Lenny.

'Of course you can't,' the boy snorted. 'I was lucky to get this – flat tyre, rusty mudguards and all. Lots of elbow grease when I get home'll make

it a bit better. Still . . .' The boy
looked at the carwash thoughtfully.

'. . . a quick eight pennyworth now
can't do any harm, can it?

He pushed the bike between the
brushes and left it propped up. He
fumbled in his pocket for money.

'A five-penny piece, a two-penny piece and a penny . . .'

'Strictly in that order,' said Lenny.

'Okay, okay . . . here goes.'

Clink-clink-clink.

Soft and slow the machine started. A cobweb of water drifted over the bike as if spun by the bristle-spiders.

'Can't even see it,' muttered the boy. 'Hope it's all right.'

The machine stopped suddenly and Lenny's mouth gaped open.

'You can see it now,' he exclaimed.

'Is *that* the bike I bought my Dad?' gasped the boy.

In the carwash was a racing-bike – with racing handlebars, racing pedals, a light-weight frame and racing fittings. It was so new it looked as if its paint had just finished drying.

'It's yours,' said Lenny. 'It must be. Won't your Dad be pleased.'

'Pleased?' said the boy faintly. 'With a brand new racing-bike? He'll have such a big grin on his face he'll have to be careful he doesn't swallow his ears! But how did it happen?'

'The carwash only did what it says it'll do,' Lenny pointed out. 'Look at the notice. "Transforms any vehicle". It's transformed your Dad's Christmas present all right.'

'It's a ruddy miracle,' the boy agreed. 'A racing-bike – for three quid!'

'And eight pence.' Lenny added.

But the boy didn't hear him. Already he was on his way home pushing the racing-bike as carefully as if it were made from fairy-dust. Perhaps it was in a way.

Parp-parp!

Lenny jumped with fright. If he'd
swung round any faster his clothes
would have been back-to-front.
Behind him this time was a car . . .
a superb car. It crouched on its tyres
like a lion about to pounce and its
bodywork was as white as a storybook
unicorn. Lenny could hear the engine
murmuring to itself – tick-over, tick-

over, tick-over, tick-over. Only a King in a crash-helmet should have driven such a car.

But the man behind the steering-wheel was nothing like a King. He was fat and frog-like. With a podgy finger, he beckoned Lenny.

'Yes, Mister?'

'I need some change, kid. Got any?'

'Not much . . . I spent most of my money on Christmas presents. Here's a five-pence piece, though . . . and a penny . . . and a two-pence piece.'

'Just what I need,' snapped the man. 'Give it here. Hurry up, kid. You're letting rain into the car.'

He snatched the coins from Lenny's hand.

'Hey,' Lenny said. 'Where's my change?'

A nasty chuckle was the only reply he got as the car slid forward.

Clink-clink-clink.

Again came a twirl of brushes and a haze of water. The car vanished. But just as suddenly as before the machine stopped.

'Wow,' exclaimed Lenny.

Into the carwash had gone a long, low sports-car built for speed and flashiness. Out of the carwash came a battered old jalopy held together by mud and string. Now the engine went sputter-clonk, sputter-clonk, sputter-clonk. From inside the wreckage came a shriek of fury.

'You saw it, kid! You saw it all! I'll have the law on whoever owns this stinking carwash. It's *destroyed* my motor! It's *ruined* it! You're a witness.'

'Well, you did get a warning, mister. Look at the notice. It says "Use it if you dare. Transforms any vehicle". You should've read it before you put the car through.'

36

'That notice wasn't there.'

'It was mister. I'm a witness.'

'Tell a lie then. I'll pay you well. Here – look at this wallet: full of fifty-pound notes. What are you shaking your head for, you stupid little brat?'

'Lying's wrong, mister.'

'You . . . you stinky little guttersnipe!'

The fat man looked like a toad having a tantrum. Snarling with rage he crashed his crock of a car into gear and sputter-clonked, sputter-clonked away.

Lenny stared at the carwash. It was the biggest he'd ever seen and also the smartest and when it was switched on it had a hum like faraway clockwork turning the world. Otherwise it was the same as any other carwash. So how could he trust what he'd just seen? Had it really happened . . . here in the backstreets of London on a Christmas Eve with rain turning to sleet and sleet turning to snow?

Yes, it was snowing now. Down and down came snowflakes from the nearly-dark sky like winter arriving by parachute. Already the ground was white with a million crystals. These muffled the clip-clop, clip-clop, clip-clop, clip-clop of horses' hooves.

Horses' hooves?

For a third time Lenny looked behind him. Over the wasteground came two horses, a cart and a rag-and-bone man.

On the back of the cart was junk –
rusty junk, bulky junk, spiky junk,
floppy junk, top-heavy junk, and
just plain junky-junk.

'Whoa-back!' called the rag-and-
bone man.

He pulled hard on the reins.
The horses snorted and came to a
stop.

'Hello, little feller,' said the
rag-and-bone man. 'Is this your
carwash?'

'No,' said Lenny.

'Ah . . . you're the manager then,
are you?'

'No, I'm just standing here.'

The rag-and-bone man scratched at
his beard. It was dirty and tangled
like the clothes he wore. He had a

dirty face, too, tangled with age. But Lenny liked him. Especially his voice. It sounded like chestnuts roasting on a fire.

'. . . "Transforms Any Vehicle",' read the rag-and-bone man. 'Does it now . . . that sounds a bargain to me. And all I need is a five-penny piece, a two-penny piece and a penny, strictly in that order. I can just about afford that, with a bit of luck. Let me see. A five and a two and a penny . . . yes. Would you mind putting them in the slot for me, little feller? Since you're just standing there?'

'Sure,' said Lenny. 'But you've got to be careful. It does say "Use it if you dare"!'

'So it does . . . so it does. *Do* I dare, then? That's the question. Would you dare, little feller?'

Lenny brushed the snowflakes from his eyes.

'Yes,' he said. 'I think I would.'

'Then jump up beside me and we'll dare together.'

'I'll put the money in first,' said Lenny.

Clink, clink, clink. On the stroke of

the third clink, Lenny hopped up on
the driver's seat next to the rag-and-
bone man and the carwash was on the
move.

Wouldn't they get wet?

It was too late for Lenny to worry.
Already the machine had gone clunk
all over and the buzzing had started.
Ahead was a spatter of water and whirl
of brushes. Were they creeping up on
the cart or was the cart
creeping up on them?

Help!

Help? Who needed help? Lenny
and the rag-and-bone man were
surrounded by bristles and pitter-
patter but they weren't soaked and
they weren't scrubbed. It was more like
being tickled by multi-coloured snow.
They couldn't see each other, nor could
they see what was happening to the
horses and the cart and the junk.

Would everything drip and glisten
when it was all over, Lenny
wondered?

At last the blizzard began to die down and Lenny had a good look.

'Yes,' he whispered. 'Everything is dripping and glistening . . . but it's not the same everything.'

There hadn't been antlers before, on the heads of magnificent reindeer.

There hadn't been a sleigh
before, with up-curving
runners of the bluest steel.
And there hadn't been presents –
presents and presents and
more presents of every
gift-wrapped shape and
size and weight. Lenny shut
his eyes tight.

'I don't believe it,' he said.
'It's just like you're told when
you're little. I'm much too
old to believe it.'

'*I'm* much to old to believe it as well,' came a roast-chestnut voice. 'Every year I tell myself that. It's time people forgot all about me. After all, who could believe in an old man who rides through the sky and can visit millions and millions of children in a single night by climbing down the chimney? Utterly daft! Anyway, what about the houses that haven't got chimneys?'

'The block of flats where I live hasn't got a single chimney,' said Lenny.

'Exactly. Keep your eyes shut, Lenny. Especially now we're on our way. One peek through those fingers and who knows what you'll start believing? Gee up, my beauties!'

'Where are we going?' asked Lenny.

'First stop – Australia. Might
even see those cousins of yours
who live in the beach-house. See
what I mean, Lenny? All this is
impossible – quite impossible.'

Lenny's eyes blinked open.

'How do you know my cousins?
And how do you know my
name?'

'That's another thing,' agreed Santa Claus. 'How *could* I know your cousins and know your name? If I were you, Lenny, I'd take the whole thing with a pinch of salt. Tell yourself you're dreaming or something. Stick to your principles.'

'But we're *here*, Santa. And it really *is* happening.'

Santa Claus chuckled. His beard was just as white as you're told when you're little and his eyes were just as blue.

'That's true, Lenny. So why not just sit back and enjoy it? You can worry about believing it later on.'

'Okay,' grinned Lenny.

And he sat back to enjoy it.

For Lenny the night was as long and as short as the best school holiday ever.

They crossed oceans and deserts, jungles and mountains. Whether in a city so big it stretched from horizon to horizon or in a place so wild you were surprised to find a home there

at all, Santa Claus still found a way
of doing his job.

Towards morning, the jingle of
sleigh bells and the clatter of reindeer
on yet another roof were too much
for Lenny. He fell asleep.

When he woke up it was Christmas.
At the foot of his bed were two
parcels. One was big – about the size
of roller-blades or a computer or a
football game. The other parcel was
small. Lenny picked up the small one
and went to the window. He pulled
back the curtains and stared across the
snow-white Council Estate and the
snow-white wasteground beyond it.

The wasteground was sad and spooky again . . . and empty.

'Where's the carwash?' Lenny wailed. 'Where's it gone? Did I dream it after all? Oh, Santa . . . I did *want* to believe in you, honest.' Sadly, he undid the small parcel. Inside was a small card and an envelope. On the card his Gran had written 'Happy Christmas, Lenny. You've already had your present from me. I wrote to Santa about it. But here's a little something for *next* year.'

When Lenny opened the envelope he found a five-penny piece, a two-penny piece and a penny. They fell into his hand strictly in that order.

Barn Owl Books

THE PUBLISHING HOUSE DEVOTED ENTIRELY TO
THE REPRINTING OF CHILDREN'S BOOKS

RECENT TITLES

Arabel's Raven – Joan Aiken
Mortimer the raven finds the Joneses and causes chaos in Rumbury Town

Mortimer's Bread Bin – Joan Aiken
Mortimer the raven is determined to sleep in the bread bin. Mrs Jones says no

The Spiral Stair – Joan Aiken
Giraffe thieves are about! Arabel and her raven have to act fast

Your Guess is as Good as Mine – Bernard Ashley
Nicky gets into a stranger's car by mistake

The Gathering – Isobelle Carmody
Four young people and a ghost battle with a strange evil force

Voyage – Adèle Geras
Story of four young Russians sailing to the U.S. in 1904

Private – Keep Out! – Gwen Grant
Diary of the youngest of six in the 1940s

Leila's Magical Monster Party – Ann Jungman
Leila invites all the baddies to her party and they come!

The Silver Crown – Robert O'Brien
A rare birthday present leads to an extraordinary quest

Playing Beatie Bow – Ruth Park
Exciting Australian time travel story in which Abigail learns about love

The Mustang Machine – Chris Powling
A magic bike sorts out the bullies

The Intergalactic Kitchen – Frank Rodgers
The Bird family plus their kitchen go into outer space

You're Thinking about Doughnuts – Michael Rosen
Frank is left alone in a scary museum at night

Jimmy Jelly – Jacqueline Wilson
A T.V. personality is confronted by his greatest fan

The Devil's Arithmetic – Jane Yolen
Hannah from New York time travels to Auschwitz in 1942 and acquires
wisdom